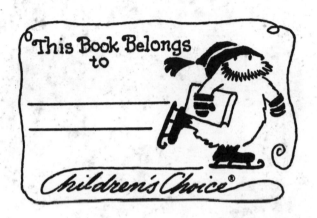

This Book Belongs to
_____
_____
Children's Choice®

JEAN DE BRUNHOFF

BABAR
AND
FATHER CHRISTMAS

Translated from the French
by Merle Haas

Random House, Inc.   New York

The Babar Books

The Story of Babar
The Travels of Babar
Babar the King
Babar and Zéphir
Babar and His Children
Babar and Father Christmas
Babar's Cousin: That Rascal Arthur
Babar's Picnic
Babar's Fair
Babar and the Professor
Babar's Castle
Babar's French Lessons
Babar Comes to America
Babar's Spanish Lessons
Babar Loses His Crown
Babar's Trunk
Babar's Birthday Surprise
Babar's Other Trunk
Babar Visits Another Planet
Meet Babar and His Family
Babar's Bookmobile
Babar and the Wully-Wully
Babar Saves the Day

Lithographed in the United States of America
Copyright, 1940, by Random House, Inc.

Copyright renewed 1968 by Random House, Inc.
and Cecil de Brunhoff
ISBN: 0-590-75786-5

One day Zéphir calls to his friends Arthur, Pom, Flora and Alexander:

"Listen, listen to this wonderful tale which I've just heard! It seems that in Man's country, every year, on the night before Christmas, a very kind old gentleman with a large white beard, wearing a red suit with a pointed hood, flies over the countryside. He carries with him great quantities of toys and gives them to the little children. They call him Father Christmas. It is difficult to catch a glimpse of him for he comes down the chimney while one sleeps. Next morning the children know he has been there because they find toys in their shoes. Why shouldn't we write to him and ask him to come here too and see us in the Elephants' country?"

"Three cheers! What a fine idea!" says Alexander. "But what shall we say in the letter?" asks Arthur. "We must write and tell Father Christmas what we would like him to bring us," suggests Pom. "Let's consider very carefully before we write," adds Flora.

They remain quiet a moment and think it over.

Zéphir decides a bicycle would be just what he wants, Flora would love to have a doll. Alexander wants a butterfly net, Pom a big bag of candies and a little Teddy Bear. As for Arthur, his dream is to have a train.

Then, each having decided what to wish for, Zéphir is chosen to write the letter, for he has the best handwriting. He applies himself to his task. Arthur remembers that a stamp must be put on the envelope. Then they each sign their names and go off together in great glee to mail the letter.

Every morning the five friends eagerly await the postman. They rush out to meet him as soon as they see him coming. But alas, although the postman searches carefully, there is no answer from Father Christmas.

One day Babar happens to see them and says to himself: "Whatever can be the matter with those children? They look so dreadfully sad."

So he calls to them
and says: "Come on, tell
me what's the matter."

Zéphir tells him the story of his letter.

"And you haven't had an answer? Is that it?" asks Babar.
"You must have forgotten to put a stamp on it."

"Oh no we didn't, Arthur remembered to."

"Well, then Father Christmas hasn't had time to answer
it yet. Cheer up and run along now and play. Possibly you've
given me a very excellent idea."

Babar paces thoughtfully up and down, lost in thought.
"I wonder why I never
thought myself
of asking Father
Christmas to come
to the Elephants'
country."

"The best thing to do
would be to start out
at once to find him.
If I ask him personally
he will surely not
refuse to come."

His mind made up, Babar hurries to inform Celeste of
his intentions. She helps him to pack and get ready. She
would like very much to go along, but Babar explains to
her that she'll be needed at home to rule the country during
his absence, and also remarks that queer characters like
Father Christmas are often shy, and rarely allow themselves
to be approached by more than one person at a time.

Babar arrives in Europe after a very good journey. He
has just stepped from the train. In order not to be recognized

he has left his crown
at home.

He drives to a little old hotel which is clean and quiet, and is given a room which pleases him. Next he undresses and washes up a bit. One always feels so refreshed after a good cleaning up. "What can be making that funny little noise?" wonders Babar as he dries himself off. Without moving he looks around, and all of a sudden he sees three young mice.

The least timid of them says: "Good-day, my stout Sir, are we to have the pleasure of your company for long?"

"Oh no, I'm just passing through. I'm looking for Father Christmas," answers Babar.

"You're looking for Father Christmas. — Why, goodness, he's here in this very house, we know him well. We'll show you his room," chorused the three little mice.

"How wonderful! What really extraordinary luck! Just give me time to put on my dressing gown, and I'll be with you," cries the excited Babar.

"But where on earth are these little mice leading me?" wonders Babar as he stops a moment on the stairs to catch his breath. "Father Christmas must live way up on the top floor. No doubt he likes to have a good view and plenty of open space around him."

While Babar is making these observations, the three little mice reach the attic. Whatever are they doing over there in that corner? They seem all excited!

"Where are you?" calls Babar.

"Up here in the attic," answer the little mice. "Come quickly! We have taken Father Christmas down from the top of the tree."

When Babar joins them, the delighted little mice say:

"There is Father Christmas! He lives here peacefully the whole year round, excepting on Christmas Day when they come and fetch him to hang on top of a new Christmas tree. After the holiday he resumes his place in this corner and we can come and play with him again."

"But this isn't the one I'm looking for; I want to find the real live Father Christmas, not a doll!" says Babar sadly.

Next morning Babar hears a tapping at his window, and sees some sparrows outside on the sill. They speak to him and say:

"We understand that you are searching for the real live Father Christmas. We know him well and are going to take you to him." And off they fly joyously.

Pointing out the way to Babar, they lead him across the big bridge over the river. "We're almost there," they call. "We usually find him around here, he sleeps under the bridges."

"Well, well, that is strange," thinks Babar.

"There he is! There he is!" cry all the little sparrows together. "He's over there next to that fisherman casting his line."

Babar, still a bit astonished at this old fellow's odd appearance, greets him and says: "Excuse me, Sir. But are you really the true Father Christmas, the one who brings toys to all the children?"

"Alas no," answers the old man. "My name is Lazzaro Campeotti. I am an artist's model and my friends the artists have nick-named me Father Christmas. Now every-body calls me by that name."

Very much disappointed, Babar strolls thoughtfully along the river banks.

Stopping at one of the book stalls, Babar finds a book with pictures of Father Christmas. He quickly buys it and takes it back to his room to examine it more carefully. Unfortunately the text is written in a language which he does not understand. He goes down to explain his difficulty to the hotel manager, who helpfully gives him the address of a professor at the school where his son is studying.

"Mr. Gillianez will surely be able to translate your book," says he.

Without losing a moment, Babar is at the door of Professor Gillianez' house ringing the bell. He finds him at home but after a glance at the book the Professor says that to his great regret he is unable to read it either. He gives Babar the address of the famous Professor William Jones.

An hour later Babar is in this man's study. The Professor carefully examines the book, and shakes his head gloomily. Finally he turns to Babar who has been waiting patiently, and says: "Your book is very difficult to read. It is written in old style Gothic letters. There are facts in it about the life of Father Christmas, and they say he lives in Bohemia, not far from the little town of PRJMNESWE. But I do not find any more definite information on this point."

Babar goes off and sits on a bench in the public park to think the matter over. The birds recognize him and come over to inquire whether he has found Father Christmas.

"No, not yet," answers Babar. "I only know that he lives far away from here near the town of PRJMNESWE. Truly this is a difficult search."

Just then a little dog who is passing by says to Babar: "Pardon me, Sir. I'm very good at finding things which are lost, because I have a highly developed sense of smell.

"If only I could have a sniff of that doll, which Father Christmas gave to little Virginia over there, I'm sure I'd be able to help you find him. I would be very glad to go with you because I am a little homeless dog."

Upon hearing these words Babar looks at the dog and says: "Agreed, I'll take you along with me."

Then off he goes to buy a beautiful new doll for Virginia which she gladly accepts in exchange for her other one. Babar lets the dog sniff the old doll, and feeds him a piece of candy.

Before starting out Babar goes back to see the learned
Professor William Jones who returns his book and gives him
a few additional directions. Father Christmas apparently
lives in a forest on a mountain about twelve miles from
PRJMNESWE.

Babar arrives at the little town after a difficult journey.

It is very cold and a great deal of snow has fallen. Babar therefore equips himself accordingly. He buys some skis, hires a sleigh and has himself driven to the foot of the mountain.

Pretty soon he has to get out and, accompanied only by his faithful Duck (this is the name he has given his dog), he starts to climb in the direction of the mysterious forest, skis on his feet, and a heavily laden pack on his back. Duck is very much excited. He sniffs here and there and yaps softly. Now he stands still, his tail lifted, his nose twitching hard. He must have caught the scent of Father Christmas.

Suddenly
Duck is
off on the run.
"I've got it!
I've got it!
We're on
the right track."
His loud
barking echoes
through the woods.
But what is that
stirring in
this wild forest?

It is a band of little mountain dwarfs who have hidden themselves behind the tree trunks. Duck would like to see them nearer by, but they rush at him, pelting him fast and furiously with hard-packed snowballs which land on his head,
in his eyes and
on his sides.

Half choked,
half blinded,
his tail
between his legs,
Duck decides
to retreat.
He quickly runs to
rejoin his master,
and arrives
breathless,
feeling very
foolish.

When Babar sees him he stops short and asks: "What's happened?" Duck then tells him of his adventure with the little bearded dwarfs.

"Good, we must be getting nearer," replies Babar. "I am very eager to meet those dwarfs, lead me to them."

A few minutes later it is Babar's turn to meet the dwarfs. They try to frighten him too, and rush bravely toward him, and pelt him, but Babar calmly takes a deep breath and blows it out hard in their direction. They all tumble down one on top of the other, and as soon as they can scramble back to their feet, off they run and noiselessly disappear.

Babar roars with laughter, and continues on his way, following Duck who has now found the scent again.

The little dwarfs have run to find Father Christmas and they tell him, all jabbering at once, that an enormous animal with a long nose blew on them so hard that he knocked them down and chased them away. Father Christmas listens attentively. The little dwarfs add that when they fled, this big monster was quite near, and that, guided by an ugly little cur, he was heading straight for the secret cave of Father Christmas.

They were right. Babar is nearing the cave, but a storm of
extraordinary violence suddenly bursts upon him. The wind blows so
hard that the snowflakes prick his eyes and skin. It is impossible to see.
Babar struggles desperately; then, realizing the danger of obstinately
forging ahead blindly, he decides to dig himself a hole for shelter.

Then he rigs up a roof with his skis and ski-poles and some snow blocks. The two companions are fairly well protected now.

"Whew! It is cold and my trunk is beginning to freeze," thinks Babar. Duck is also cold and tired.

All of a sudden, Babar feels the earth giving away under him, and he and Duck drop out of sight. Where have they fallen?

Without realizing it they have dropped right down through a chimney vent into the cave of Father Christmas. "Father Christmas!" cries the amazed Babar. "Duck, we've arrived at our destination."

Whereupon he faints, worn out with fatigue, the cold and the excitement. "Quick, little mountain dwarfs, forget your quarrel, we must undress him and get him warm," says Father Christmas.

They all set to immediately. They undress him, and give him a good alcohol rub, working over him energetically with big brushes. The dwarf chemist gives him some brandy. Then finally, Babar drinks a fine bowl of hot soup with Father Christmas and thanks him from the bottom of his heart.

While Father Christmas shows him around, Babar explains that he has made this long journey to ask him to visit the Elephants' country.

N.B.—This tour includes the big room in which Father Christmas usually lives; the room into which Babar fell through the hole, which one can see in the upper right-hand corner; and the toy rooms, the doll room, the tin soldier room, the armory with toy guns, the room full of

Won't he distribute toys to the elephant children, just as he does to
the children of men? Father Christmas is much touched by this request,

trains, the room with building blocks, the room where the stuffed animals are kept, the one with
tennis racquets and balls, etc. (all these things neatly packed in boxes and in bags). And then
they visited the dwarfs' dormitories, the elevators worked by pulleys and the machine shop.

but he tells Babar that he will not be able to visit the Elephants' country Christmas night because he is very tired.

He adds: "I had great difficulty last year in completing the usual delivery and distribution of toys to the children all over the world."

"Oh, Father Christmas, I understand perfectly," says Babar, "but if this is the case you must take care of yourself.

"Why not live on the earth's surface for a while and leave your underground home? Come back with me now to our country and bask in the sun. You will be rested and cured for Christmas."

Charmed by this suggestion, Father Christmas instructs the little dwarfs to keep an eye on everything for him. Then off he goes in his flying machine, accompanied by Babar and Duck.

Here they are in the Elephants' country. Father Christmas admires the countryside and is quickly surrounded by the elephants who rush over to bid him welcome. Pom, Flora and Alexander hurry over too. In order to get the best view, Arthur has climbed to the roof of a house and Zéphir is up in a tree.

When the excitement quiets down Queen Celeste introduces her three children and Arthur and Zéphir to Father Christmas. "Oh, you are the ones who wrote me," he says. "I am delighted to meet you and I promise you a Merry Christmas."

Father Christmas
often goes
out riding
on zebra back.
Babar rides
along on
his bicycle.
And Father Christmas takes a sun-bath for two full hours every day, following Dr. Capoulosse's instructions. Sometimes Pom, Flora and Alexander come to watch him as he lies in his hammock, but they are careful to make no noise, so as not to disturb him.

One day
Father Christmas
says to Babar:
"My dear friend,
thank you very
much for all that you
have done for me.

Christmas is nearly here and I must leave to distribute the awaited gifts to the children of men. But I'm not forgetting the promise I made to the little elephants. Can you guess what I have in this bag? A real Santa Claus suit made to your measure! It is a magic suit which will enable you to fly through the air, and your bag will always be full of toys. You can take my place here Christmas Eve. I promise you I'll return when my work is done and I'll bring the children a fine Christmas tree."

On the night before Christmas Babar follows out these instructions. As soon as he puts on the suit and beard, he notices that he instantly becomes lighter and is at the same time able to fly with ease.

"This is really extraordinary! And what a good way to distribute all the gifts to the children!" thinks Babar.

He hurries in order to get through with his task before dawn. What joy there will be in every house on Christmas morning when the little elephants awake!

In the royal palace Queen Celeste peeks through the door of the children's room. Pom is emptying his stocking, Flora is rocking her doll, and Alexander is jumping up and down on his bed, exclaiming: "What a wonderful Christmas! What a wonderful Christmas!"

As he had promised, Father Christmas has come back bringing them a beautiful Christmas tree. And thanks to him the family celebration is a great success.

Arthur, Zéphir, Pom, Flora and Alexander have never seen anything as beautiful as this fir tree all shining with lights.

Next day, Father Christmas flies away again in his airplane to rejoin his little subjects, the dwarfs, in his underground palace.

On the banks of the big lake, Babar, Celeste, Arthur, Zéphir, and the three children sadly wave their handkerchiefs.

Fortunately, Father Christmas has promised to come back to the Elephants' country every year.

Look Who's Part of the Children's Choice® Family!

Something special for Children's Choice® Book Club members

You can get all these storybook favorites—Puss in Boots, Babar, Curious George, Lyle, George and Martha and The Year at Maple Hill Farm—to hang up on your wall. They're big (17" × 22") and beautiful posters, printed in full color on high quality paper. Best of all, you can get all 6 for just $3.95, including postage and handling.

To order your set of 6 Children's Choice® posters, please send your name, address and $3.95 in check or money order to:

CHILDREN'S CHOICE®POSTERS
2931 East McCarty St.
P.O. Box 1068
Jefferson City, Mo. 65102

Please allow 3-6 weeks for delivery. Your posters are mailed in a tube, so they won't be creased at all.

Offer expires January 15, 1980